KIDNAPPED

诱　拐

作者　罗伯特·路易斯·斯蒂文森

改编　保琳·弗兰西斯

译者　杨秋红

主编　刘启萍

青岛出版社

图书在版编目(CIP)数据

诱拐(英汉对照)/(英)斯蒂文森著;(英)弗兰西斯改编;
杨秋红译. —青岛:青岛出版社,2008.1
(外国文学名著快听快读系列)
ISBN 978-7-5436-4618-6

Ⅰ.诱… Ⅱ.①斯… ②弗… ③杨… Ⅲ.①英语—汉语—
对照读物 ②长篇小说—英国—近代 Ⅳ.H319.4:Ⅰ

中国版本图书馆 CIP 数据核字(2007)第 200904 号

First published by Evans Brothers Limited
2A Portman Mansions, Chiltern Street, London W1U 6NR, United Kingdom
Copyright © Cherrytree Books year as it is printed in the UK edition
This edition published under licence from Evans Brothers Ltd.
All rights reserved

山东省版权局著作权合同登记号   图字:15-2007-069 号

书　　名	诱拐	
作　　者	罗伯特·路易斯·斯蒂文森	
改　　编	保琳·弗兰西斯	
译　　者	杨秋红	
出版发行	青岛出版社	
社　　址	青岛市徐州路 77 号,266071	
本社网址	http://www.qdpub.com	
邮购电话	(0532)85814750　85840228	
责任编辑	曹永毅　王超明　**E-mail**:cyyx2001@sohu.com	
封面设计	杨津津	
照　　排	青岛正方文化传播有限公司	
印　　刷	青岛新新华印刷有限公司	
出版日期	2008 年 1 月第 1 版　2008 年 1 月第 1 次印刷	
开　　本	16 开(715mm×1000mm)	
印　　张	4	
字　　数	70 千	
书　　号	ISBN 978-7-5436-4618-6	
定　　价	11.00 元	

编校质量、盗版监督电话　(0532)80998671

青岛版图书售出后如发现印装质量问题,请寄回青岛出版社印刷物资处调换。
电话:(0532)80998826

Kidnapped

Introduction

Robert Louis Stevenson was born in 1850, in Edinburgh, Scotland. After studying law at Edinburgh University, he decided to earn his living as a writer. Unfortunately, he became ill with tuberculosis, a disease of the lungs, and he had to travel to warmer countries to improve his health.

In 1880, Robert Louis Stevenson married Fanny Osborne and a year later, he wrote *Treasure Island* for her young son. In 1886, *Kidnapped* was published. Both these books were very popular, but they did not make much money. So, in 1886, Stevenson wrote *The Strange Case of Dr Jekyll and Mr Hyde*. This story made Stevenson well known, and made him more money, because it was bought by adults.

Kidnapped is a story of the kidnapping of David Balfour, a young boy who is cheated out of his inheritance and wrongly accused of murder. It is set in 1751, five years after the Jacobites (led by Bonnie Prince Charlie, the son of James II) were defeated at Culloden Moor in the north of Scotland. The Jacobites supported James II, who claimed the right to be the king of Great Britain, instead of King George. Most of the Scottish Highlanders were loyal Jacobites and had their land taken from them by King George.

In 1887, Stevenson's father died. With the money he left, Robert Louis Stevenson and his family were able to live in Samoa, an island in the Pacific Ocean. The warm climate improved his health and he wrote there until his death in 1894.

You might find the meaning of these words will help you to understand the story better:

ay(e)	yes
brae	hill
burn	stream
clan	group of families with the same family name
crofter	a farmer
dirk	dagger
Gaelic	a Celtic language
glen	mountain valley
The Highlands	a large area of north and north-east Scotland
Jacobite	a supporter of James Stuart who wanted to rule Britain
ken	know
laird	a Scottish landowner
loch	lake
The Lowlands	the central and eastern part of Scotland
nae	no, not
Redcoats	British soldiers (they wore scarlet jackets)
ye	you

罗伯特·路易斯·斯蒂文森1850年生于苏格兰的爱丁堡。 他毕业于爱丁堡大学的法律系，后来决心以写作为生。 很不幸，他患了肺结核，不得不到气候温暖的国家以改善健康状况。

1880年，罗伯特·路易斯·斯蒂文森与范妮·奥斯波恩结婚。 一年后，斯蒂文森为她的小儿子创作了《金银岛》，1886年又出版了《诱拐》。 这两本书深受读者的喜爱，却未能使他赚到很多钱。 于是1886年，他又写出《化身博士》。 该书使斯蒂文森声名大振，也为他赚取了更多的钱，因为书出售给了成年人。

《诱拐》一书讲述了少年戴维·鲍尔弗被诱拐的全过程，他不仅受骗丢了遗产而且被人诬陷为杀人犯。 故事发生在1751年，5年前詹姆斯党人（首领为詹姆斯二世之子邦尼·查理王子）在苏格兰北部的卡洛登沼地惨遭溃败，他们支持自称为英国合法国王的詹姆斯二世，反对乔治国王。 许多苏格兰高地部族都是忠实的詹姆斯党人，他们被乔治国王赶出了家园。

1887年，斯蒂文森的父亲去世。 凭借父亲留下的钱，罗伯特·路易斯·斯蒂文森才得以和家人住在太平洋中的萨摩亚岛上。 岛上温暖的气候改善了他的健康状况，他在那里潜心写作，直到1894年去世。

你可能会发现，了解这些词的意思，将帮你更好地理解故事：

ay(e)	是的
brae	小山
burn	小溪
clan	具有相同姓氏的家族群
crofter	佃农
dirk	匕首
Gaelic	盖尔语

glen	山谷
The Highlands	苏格兰北部和东北广阔地域
Jacobite	詹姆斯·斯图亚特的支持者，詹姆斯想统治英国
ken	知道
laird	苏格兰庄园主
loch	湖泊
The Lowlands	苏格兰中部和东部
nae	不，不是
Redcoats	英国士兵（他们穿着深红色外套）
ye	你

CHAPTER ONE

The House of Shaws

*T*he story of kidnap and murder that you are about to read began one June morning in 1751. I was only seventeen and both my parents had just died. I decided to leave Essendean, the village where I had always lived, and seek my fortune in the world. The minister of Essendean, Mr Campbell, came to see me before I left.

"I have something for ye, lad," he said. "When your father was ill, he gave this letter to me. Ye are to take it to the house of Shaws, near Edinburgh."

I looked at him in surprise.

"The Balfours of Shaws is an old and respected family — your family," he told me. "That is where your father came from and he wanted you to go back there."

He gave me the letter addressed in my father's handwriting:

To Ebenezer Balfour, Esquire,
the house of Shaws
to be delivered by my son, David Balfour

"Remember, Davie," Mr Campbell said, "that Ebenezer Balfour is the laird and you must obey him."

"I'll try, sir," I said.

"Now you must go," Mr Campbell said sadly, "you have two days walking ahead of you."

I took my last look at the churchyard where my mother and father were buried, then I began my journey. How pleased I was to be leaving the quiet countryside to go to a great and busy house, among rich people of my own family!

In the middle of the second day, I caught sight of the sea from the top of a hill — and the great city of Edinburgh. I was very excited, but when I started to ask the way to the house of Shaws, people looked at me in surprise.

"If ye'll take my advice," one man said sharply, "ye'll keep away from the Shaws."

At first, I wanted to turn back.

"No!" I told myself firmly, "now that I've come so far, I have to find out for myself."

Just as the sun began to set, I met an old woman trudging down a hill.

"Am I far from the house of Shaws?" I asked her.

She took me back up the hill and pointed to the valley below.

"That is the house of Shaws!" she said angrily. "Blood built it. Blood stopped the building of it. Blood will be its ruin. I spit upon the ground and curse Ebenezer Balfour!"

I was frightened by her words, but I forced myself to walk up to the house. The nearer I got, the gloomier it seemed. There was no gate and no avenue — and one wing of the house was unfinished. Was this the fine house my father was sending me to? Was this where I was going to earn my fortune?

I knocked once on the wooden door. There was silence. I waited and knocked again. Then I felt angry and shouted, "Mr Balfour! Mr Ebenezer Balfour!" until a man called from the bedroom window above my head.

"It's loaded."

I looked up into the mouth of a gun.

"I've come here with a letter," I said, "to Mr Ebenezer Balfour of the house of Shaws. Is he here?"

"Ye can put it down upon the doorstep, and be off with ye," the man said.

"No!" I cried. "I will deliver it into Mr. Balfour's hands. It is a letter of introduction. I am David Balfour."

There was a long pause.

"Is your father dead?" the man asked at last.

I was too upset to answer.

"Ay," the man said, "he'll be dead. I'll let you in."

After a few minutes, a stooping man of about fifty opened the door. His face was grey and mean, and he had a long beard trailing onto his nightshirt. He led me down a corridor to a cold, dark kitchen.

"Let me see the letter," he said.

"It's for Mr Balfour," I answered.

"And who do ye think I am?" he said. "Now give me Alexander's letter."

"You know my father's name?" I asked in surprise.

"It would be strange if I didnae," the man said, "for he was my younger brother."

"I never knew, sir, that he had a brother," I said, my voice trembling.

I slept badly that night, locked in a cold bedroom with broken window-panes, but the next day my uncle seemed friendlier. In the evening, when we had eaten some porridge together, he lit a pipe and leaned towards me across the table.

"Davie, my man," he said, "I'm going to help ye as your father wanted. I kept a bit of money for ye, since ye were born — not much — well, forty pounds!"

I was too surprised to say anything.

"I want nae thanks," he said. "I do my duty. But I want ye to do something for me. There's a chest in the tower at the far end of the house, the part that's not finished. Bring it down for me."

"Can I have a candle, sir?" I asked.

"Nae lights in my house," he told me.

I went outside. It was darker than ever. My heart pounded as I climbed the steps to the top of the tower, feeling the wall with my hands. Suddenly, there was a flash of lightning and I looked down in horror. The unfinished staircase came to an end there, high in the air.

"One more step and I would have fallen!" I gasped.

Then the terrible thought came into my mind.

"My uncle sent me here to die!"

第一章　肖　家

你将要读到的这个诱拐和谋杀的故事始于 1751 年 6 月的一个上午。那年我只有 17 岁，父母都已过世，我决定离开久居的埃森底村到外面闯荡一番。 我临行前，埃森底的牧师坎贝尔先生来见了我一面。

"小伙子，我有东西给你。"他说，"你父亲生病时托付给我这封信。你要拿着它去爱丁堡附近的肖家。"

我吃惊地看着他。

"姓鲍尔弗的肖家是一个古老、受人尊敬的家庭——是你家。"他告诉我，"你父亲生于那个家庭，他希望你回去。"

他递给我信，信封上是父亲的笔迹：

埃比尼泽·鲍尔弗先生亲启，

肖家

此信由我儿戴维·鲍尔弗亲自投送

"记牢，戴维，"坎贝尔先生说，"埃比尼泽·鲍尔弗是田庄的主人，你一定要服从他。"

"我会尽力的，先生。"我回答。

"现在你得起程了。"坎贝尔先生悲伤地说，"你要走两天的路才能到。"

我最后望了一眼葬着父母的教堂墓地，便踏上了行程。 我内心多么高兴啊，因为可以离开冷清的乡下，到一个热闹的大家庭去，还能跟那些有钱的本家人在一起！

第二天中午，我从一座山岗的顶上望到了大海——还有宏伟的爱丁堡城。 我非常兴奋，但向人们打听怎样去肖家时，他们却投来吃惊的目光。

"如果你愿意接受我的建议，"有人严厉地说，"请远离肖家。"

起初，我想打道回府。

"不行！"我坚定地对自己说，"既然已经走了这么远，那我非自己找到不可。"

正当夕阳西下，我碰到一个老妇人，她正疲惫地从一座小山上走下。

"我离肖家还远吗？"我问她。

她带我爬回山头，指向下边的山谷。

"那就是肖家！"她愤愤地说，"它是用鲜血建造的，鲜血阻止过它的建造，鲜血还会将其毁灭。 我唾弃并诅咒埃比尼泽·鲍尔弗！"

我被她的话语吓了一跳，但还是强制自己走向了肖家。 离得越近，它越发显得阴郁，没有大门和道路——房屋的一个侧楼还未建好。 难道这就是父亲让我投奔的豪宅吗？ 难道我就在此谋生吗？

我敲了敲木门，里面却一片寂静。 我等了等，再次敲门。 我生气了，嚷道："鲍尔弗先生！ 埃比尼泽·鲍尔弗先生！"一个男人在我头顶上的卧室窗口喊道：

"它可装了子弹。"

我抬头正对着枪口。

"我带着信来这儿的，"我说，"要交给肖家的埃比尼泽·鲍尔弗先生。 他在吗？"

"你可以把信放到门口台阶上，马上离开！"那人说。

"不行！"我叫道，"我要把信亲自交到鲍尔弗先生手中。 这是一封介绍信。 我是戴维·鲍尔弗。"

很长时间没有回音。

"你父亲死了吗？"那人终于问道。

我难过得无法回答。

"啊，"他说，"他肯定死了，我让你进来吧。"

几分钟后，一个弯腰驼背的50来岁老人开了门。 他面色苍白，神情卑贱，胡须长得可以触到睡衣。 沿着过道，他把我领进了又冷又黑的厨房里。

"让我看看信。"他说。

"是给鲍尔弗先生的。"我回答。

"那么，你以为我是谁呀？"他说，"现在把亚历山大的信给我。"

"你知道我父亲的名字？"我吃惊地问。

"我不知道才算奇怪呢，"那人说，"他可是我弟弟啊。"

"先生，我一直不知父亲还有个哥哥。"我声音颤抖着说道。

那夜我睡得很差，因为我被锁在一间窗玻璃已破碎的冰冷卧室里。 但是第二天，叔叔显得友好起来。 晚上我们一块喝稀饭时，他点起烟斗，身子隔着桌子探向我。

"戴维，我的孩子，"他说，"如你父亲所愿，我会帮你的。 你出生后，我为你存了点钱——不多——嗯，40英镑！"

我吃惊得一句话也说不出来。

"我不要感谢。"他说，"这是我应做的，不过我想让你办件事。 有个箱子在这幢房子最尽头的顶楼上，也就是未建好的那部分，给我把它拿下来。"

"我能点根蜡烛吗，先生？"我问。

"我的房内不准有光。"他告诉我。

我走到外面，天色比以往都要黑。 沿着台阶爬向顶楼时，我用手摸着墙壁，心里扑通扑通直跳。 突然，一阵电光闪过，我害怕地向下望去。未建成的台阶已到尽头，高耸在空中。

"再迈一步，我可能就已经掉下去了！"我倒吸一口气。

然后，我脑中掠过一个可怕的想法。

"叔叔让我来这儿送死啊！"

CHAPTER TWO

Kidnapped!

I came slowly down the steps again and went back to the kitchen. When I crept up behind my uncle and put my hands on his shoulders, he fell to the floor like a dead man.

"Sit up!" I shouted.

"Are ye alive?" my uncle sobbed. "O man. Are ye alive?"

"I am," I said, "no thanks to you. Why did you try to kill me?"

"I'll talk to ye in the morning," my uncle moaned, "I feel too ill right now."

I locked my uncle in his room. Then I lit the biggest fire the house had seen for years and fell asleep. In the morning, as I was deciding what to do, a ship's boy called Ransome brought a letter for my uncle.

"It's from Captain Hoseason," my uncle said. "He's just sailed into Queensferry port. He wants to see me."

I shook my head.

"I've treated ye badly, Davie," he said. "If ye let me see the captain, I'll take ye to see my lawyer, Mr Rankeillor in Queensferry. He knew your father. We'll sort out some money for ye."

"I do want to see the sea," I thought. "I'll go, but I won't let my uncle out of my sight."

We followed Ransome to an inn alongside the port. The room where my uncle and Hoseason talked was so hot that I left them for a few minutes to look at the ships. When I returned, my uncle was coming downstairs with Captain Hoseason.

"Ye shall come on board my ship for half-an-hour," the captain smiled, "just until the tide comes in, and have a drink with me."

"No thank you," I said, "we're on our way to see Mr Rankeillor."

"I know that," the captain said, "and I can stop at Queensferry pier, a stone's throw from the lawyer's house." He bent over and whispered in my ear. "Be careful of your uncle, he's a cunning old fox. Perhaps I can help ye."

I thought I had found a friend.

We went over to the ship in a rowing boat. I boarded the ship first with the captain and waited for my uncle to come on board. There was no sign of him.

"Where's my uncle?" I asked at last.

The captain did not answer. I looked down at the rowing boat below and saw my uncle rowing back to the shore. I shouted, "Help! Help!" until I felt a hard blow on the back of my head. Then I fell down onto the deck.

When I came round again, I was lying in the pitch black, tied up and in great pain. I heard the roaring of the sea, the thundering of the sails and the shouts of the seamen. My whole world heaved up and down. I trembled with fear and despair. I did not know whether it was night or day in that evil-smelling ship where rats pattered across my face.

"They've kidnapped me!" I whispered to myself.

I think I would have died if the second officer, Mr Riach, had not taken me up on the deck. In the fresh air, I began to feel better. I told Mr Riach what had happened.

　　"I will do my best to help ye, lad," he said. "But ye're not the only one this has happened to."

　　"Where are we?" I asked.

　　"Between the Orkney and the Shetland Islands," he told me. "In a few days, we'll be going round the north coast of Scotland."

　　"Then where?" I whispered.

　　"America," Mr Riach replied.

　　I slowly began to feel stronger and I began to think of ways to escape. But as that became less and less likely, I imagined what my new life would be like if I was a slave in a strange country. About a week later, the captain came looking for me.

"Davie, lad," he said kindly, "we want ye to go and work up in the roundhouse instead of Ransome. "

"But what about Ransome?" I asked, jumping out of my bunk.

As I spoke, a man put Ransome in my bunk. I looked at the boy's white face and my blood ran cold. I knew that he was dead.

The roundhouse stood six feet high above the ship's deck. Inside were bunks for the captain, Mr Riach and Mr Shuan, the first officer. Most of the food and drink and guns were also kept here. Light came from a small skylight. I listened as I served these men, and I learned that it was Mr Shuan who had beaten poor Ransome to death.

On the tenth day after my kidnapping, near the Hebrides, we sailed into a thick, white fog. At ten o' clock that evening, there was a loud noise.

"We've hit something!" the captain yelled.

We all rushed to the side of the ship and looked down. We had cut a small boat in two. Only one man had escaped by clinging to the bow of our ship. We pulled him aboard and took him to the roundhouse.

The stranger was small and nimble. His sunburnt face was freckled and pitted with smallpox scars. When he took off his overcoat, he took a pair of pistols from the pockets and laid them on the table. A fine sword hung from his belt. His clothes were elegant — a feathered hat, black velvet breeches and a blue, silver-buttoned coat edged with lace.

"I was on my way to France," the stranger said. "If ye can take me there, I'll pay ye well. "

"Ye've a French soldier's coat upon your back, and a Scottish tongue in your head," the captain said. "Are ye a Jacobite?"

"Are ye?" the stranger asked.

"No!" the captain answered sternly, "not me. I'm for King George."

"Will ye take me to France?" the stranger asked again.

"No," the captain said, "but I can take ye back to where ye came from."

"Very well," the stranger said. "I'll give ye well if ye take me to Loch Linnhe."

They shook hands and Captain Hoseason went onto the deck to tell his men. I stood alone with the stranger, my heart beating with excitement. I had heard many stories of exiled Jacobites coming back to Scotland from France to fetch money from their supporters in the Highlands. Was this man one of them standing right in front of me with a belt of golden guineas around his waist?

"Are you a Jacobite?" I asked him.

"Ay," he said. "And are ye for King George?"

"I don't know," I said, not wanting to annoy him.

"Bring me some more wine," the Jacobite said, holding out an empty bottle.

I left the roundhouse to fetch the key for the store room. As I came closer to the captain and his men, I felt that something was wrong. I crept up behind them and listened.

"We'll kill the Jacobite and..." the captain stopped speaking as I stepped forward.

"Captain," I said, "will you give me the key to the store room?"

"Now, Davie," Mr Riach said, "that Jacobite Highlander in there is the enemy of King George. I want ye to bring out a pistol or two for us. "

I made my way slowly back to the roundhouse. What should I do? These seamen were cruel thieves. They had kidnapped me from my own country. They had killed poor Ransome. Now they would kill the Jacobite stranger. What if I helped him?

I went into the roundhouse and stared at the Jacobite. And there and then, I made up my mind.

"They're all murderers on this ship!" I cried. "Now it's your turn!"

"My name is Alan Breck of the house of Stewart," he said quickly. "Will ye fight with me, lad?"

"I'm not a thief or a murderer — I'm David Balfour, of the house of Shaws. Yes, I'll fight with you!" I said.

第二章　我被拐卖了！

我慢慢爬下台阶，回到厨房，蹑手蹑脚地走到叔叔身后，双手放在他肩头。 他滚倒在地，像一个死人。

"坐起来吧！"我喊道。

"你还活着？"叔叔呜咽着，"哦，孩子，你还活着呀？"

"是啊，"我说，"不必感谢你吧！ 为什么要杀害我？"

"明早再跟你讲。"叔叔悲叹道，"我现在病得很重。"

我把叔叔锁到他房间，点起了火，这屋里从未有过这样旺的火。 我便睡着了。 第二天早晨，我正认真考虑该怎么办，一个叫兰赛姆的船上侍童给叔叔拿来一封信。

"霍西森船长寄来的信。"叔叔说，"他刚刚驶入皇后码头，想见见我。"

　　我摇了摇头。

　　"我曾对你不好，戴维。"他说，"如果你让我见见船长，我就带你去见我的律师，皇后码头的兰基勒先生。 他认识你的父亲，我们将为你解决钱的问题。"

　　"我的确想看看大海，"我心想，"去吧，但我不能让叔叔离开我的视线。"

　　我们跟着兰赛姆来到码头边的一家客栈。 叔叔和霍西森谈话的屋里很热，我离开几分钟去观望船只。 我要回去时，叔叔和船长正走下楼梯。

　　"你可以到船上待半个钟头，"船长笑着说，"等到涨潮，跟我喝上一杯。"

　　"不了，谢谢你，"我说，"我们还要去见兰基勒先生。"

　　"我知道，"船长说，"我会停靠在皇后码头，那里离兰基勒律师家就一箭之遥。"他俯下身对我耳语，"当心你叔叔，他可是个狡猾的老狐狸，或许我能帮助你。"

　　我以为找到了一个朋友。

　　我们划着小船来到大船旁。 我先跟船长上了大船，然后等待叔叔上船，他却没露面。

　　"我叔叔在哪里？"我终于问道。

　　船长不做声。 我低头看看小船，叔叔正划着小船驶向岸边。 我呼喊着："救我！ 救我！"随后我感到后脑勺被重重击了一下，便倒在了甲板上。

　　醒来时，我躺在一片漆黑中，手脚被捆，浑身疼痛，耳边响着海水的咆哮声、船帆的猎猎作响声和水手的喊叫声。 整个世界起起伏伏，恐惧和绝望令我颤抖，我已无法分辨白天与黑夜。 船上臭气熏天，老鼠在我脸上窜来窜去。

　　"他们把我拐卖了！"我低声自语。

　　如果不是船上的二副雷契先生把我抬上甲板，我想我可能已经死了。在新鲜空气中，我开始觉得好起来，便告诉雷契先生发生过的一切。

　　"我会尽力帮你，孩子。"他说，"并非只是你自己有这样的遭遇。"

　　"我们到哪儿了？"我问。

"奥克尼群岛和设得兰群岛之间，"他告诉我，"未来几天我们要一直沿着苏格兰北海岸前行。"

"去哪里？"我低声说。

"美洲。"雷契先生回答。

我逐渐恢复了力气，开始设法逃跑。但是，随着逃跑越来越不可能实现，我便想象如果自己在异国当奴隶，我的新生活会是什么样子。大约一周后，船长来找我。

"戴维，伙计，"他温和地说，"我们想让你代替兰赛姆去后甲板室工作。"

"那么兰赛姆干什么呢？"我边问边从床铺上跳下来。

我正问着，有人把兰赛姆放到了我的床铺上。看到他苍白的脸，我的血液都冷了。我知道他死了。

后甲板室高出船的甲板 6 英尺，里面是船长、雷契先生和大副舒安先生的床铺，大部分食物、饮品和枪支也放在里面。光亮从一扇小天窗透进来。服侍他们时，我从他们的谈话中得知，可怜的兰赛姆是被大副舒安打死的。

我被拐的第 10 天，我们在赫布里底群岛附近遇上了白色的浓雾。晚上 10 点，船发出一声巨响。

"我们撞到什么东西了！"船长嚷道。

我们都跑到船边向下望。我们的船已经把一艘小船劈成了两半，唯有一人抓住了我们船头的斜桅获救。我们把他拉上船，带入后甲板室。

陌生人身材矮小，行动敏捷，被太阳晒黑的脸上长着雀斑，布满麻点。脱掉外衣时，他从口袋中掏出一对手枪放到桌上。一把漂亮的宝剑挂在他的腰带上，他的衣服也很华丽——一顶插羽毛的帽子，黑丝绒裤子，饰有银纽扣和蕾丝花边的蓝色上衣。

"我正前往法国，"陌生人说，"如果你们能带我去那儿，我将好好酬谢你们。"

"你穿着法国士兵的衣服，却说着苏格兰话，"船长说，"你是詹姆斯党人吗？"

"你是吗？"陌生人问。

"不！"船长严肃地回答，"我不是，我支持乔治国王。"

"你能把我带到法国吗？"陌生人再次问道。

"不能，"船长说，"但我可以把你带回出发地。"

"好啊，"陌生人说，"如果你能带我到林尼湾，我将好好酬谢你。"

他们握手成交后，霍西森船长走到甲板上去告诉他的手下。我独自和陌生人站在一起，内心挺兴奋。我听说过很多关于流亡的詹姆斯党人的故事，他们从法国回到苏格兰，从他们在苏格兰高地的支持者那里收集钱财。莫非这个站在我面前腰带上挂着金币的人就是其中之一吗？

"你是詹姆斯党人吗？"我问他。

"是啊。"他说。"你支持乔治国王吗？"

"不知道。"我说道，不想惹他不高兴。

"再来点酒吧。"这位詹姆斯党人边说边扬了扬一个空空的酒瓶。

我离开后甲板室去取储藏室的钥匙。快接近船长和副手们时，我觉得事情不对劲，于是悄悄地跟在他们身后听其说话。

"我们要杀了这个詹姆斯党人，然后……"船长见我走近便打住了。

"船长，"我说，"你能给我储藏室的钥匙吗？"

"听着，戴维。"雷契先生说，"那个苏格兰高地的詹姆斯党人是乔治国王的敌人。我想让你给我们拿出一两把手枪来。"

我慢步走向后甲板室。我该怎么做呢？这些水手是残酷的盗贼。他们把我拐出了家乡，杀死了可怜的兰赛姆，现在又要谋害这个陌生的詹姆斯党人。如果我帮了他，会怎样呢？

我走进后甲板室，注视着那个詹姆斯党人。就在那一瞬间，我拿定了主意。

"船上的人都是杀人犯！"我叫道，"现在轮到杀你了！"

"我是斯图亚特家的艾伦·布雷克。"他说得很快，"你会跟我一起作战吗，孩子？"

"我不是盗贼，也不是杀人犯——我是肖家的戴维·鲍尔弗。当然，我跟你一起作战！"我说。

CHAPTER THREE

The Siege of the Roundhouse

"**Y**our job is to watch the door," Alan said. "If they try to open it, ye shoot. Climb on the bed and watch the window at the same time. How many are they?"

"Fifteen," I told him.

Alan whistled in surprise. By now, the captain and his men were tired of waiting for me to come back with the guns. Suddenly, Captain Hoseason appeared in the doorway. Alan pointed his sword at him.

"The sooner we fight, the sooner ye'll feel this sword through your body!" he cried.

The captain said nothing to Alan, but gave me an ugly look.

"I'll remember this, Davie lad," he said.

The next moment, he had gone. Alan pulled out a dirk with his left hand.

"Keep your head," he said, "for there's no going back now, lad."

I climbed up to the window, clutching a handful of pistols. My heart was beating like a bird's, faintly and quickly. I felt no hope, only an anger against the world. The attack came all of a sudden — a rush of feet, a roar, a shout from Alan, then the clash of swords as he fought with Mr Shuan.

"He killed Ransome!" I shouted.

"Watch the window!" Alan shouted back.

As he spoke, he plunged his sword into Shuan's body.

I looked through the window and saw five men running past with a large piece of wood. They tried to break down the door with it. I took a deep breath and fired at them. I must have hit one of them because the other four stopped running. I shot twice more and they ran away. Now the roundhouse was full of smoke from my pistols. Alan stood waiting, his sword covered with blood.

Suddenly, more men rushed against the door. At the same time, the glass of the skylight shattered and a man leaped through. I was too afraid to shoot. I hit him over the back of the head with a pistol but he tried to grab hold of me. My courage came back and I shot him. Then I shot another man at the skylight and he fell on top of his friend.

There were more men in the doorway. Alan's sword flashed, and every flash was followed by a man's scream, until the rest of the men ran away. Alan pushed the four dead seamen out of the roundhouse with his sword.

I could hardly breathe. The sight of the two men I had shot flashed in front of me like a nightmare. I began to sob like a child.

"Ye're a brave lad, David," Alan said kindly, "and I love ye like a brother. Sleep now. I'll take the first watch."

In the morning, Alan cut one of the silver buttons from his coat.

"I give ye this for last night's work," he said. "And wherever ye show this button, the friends of Alan Breck will help ye."

As he finished speaking, Mr Riach called out to us.

"The Captain wants to speak to the Jacobite!"

Alan went over to the window.

"Take me to Loch Linnhe as we agreed!" Alan called out angrily.

"Ay," Hoseason said, "but my Shuan is dead, thanks to ye two. None of us ken this dangerous coast, like he did. Can ye show us the way?"

"I'm more of a fighting man than a sailorman," Alan answered, "but I ken something of this land. I'll help ye."

We exchanged a bottle of brandy for two buckets of water, and the meeting came to an end. Alan and I sat all day long, exchanging stories. To my amazement, he told me that he had joined the British army because he had no money. He had later deserted and joined the Jacobites.

"Dear, oh dear," I said, "the punishment for desertion is death. Why have you come back to Scotland? Have you come to collect money?"

"I miss my friends and my country," Alan sighed. "I want to see the heather and the deer. But ye guess right, Davie. I'm here to collect money for Ardshiel, the captain of my clan. He fled to France when the Jacobites were beaten at the battle of Culloden. His Highland crofters now have to pay rent to King George, but they still send rent to Ardshiel."

"They pay their rent twice!" I said in surprise. "How loyal they must be!"

I told Alan a little about myself, and how Mr Campbell had given me my father's letter.

"I would do nothing to help a Campbell," Alan said angrily. "They've fought my clan for many years, and taken their land. I hate Colin Campbell more than all the others. We call him the Red Fox because of his red hair..."

Alan stopped for a moment as if he were too angry to speak.

"When Ardshiel fled to France," Alan continued, "Red Fox asked King George if he could collect the rent for Ardshiel's land. Now he's slowly getting rid of all Ardshiel's crofters. If ever I have the time to hunt him down, I..."

Alan said no more.

We didn't talk about it again that day. Later that night, under a cold and clear sky, the ship struck some rocks. The sea came over the deck and we could hear the ship breaking up under our feet.

"Where are we?" I shouted to Alan above the roaring waves.

"Off the coast of Mull," he shouted back. "Campbell country."

Before I could speak again, an enormous wave lifted the ship up and threw me into the sea.

第三章 围攻后甲板室

"你的职责是盯好门。"艾伦说,"如果他们试图开门,你就开枪。爬到床上,同时看好窗户。 他们有多少人呢?"

"15个。"我告诉他。

艾伦吃惊地吹起了口哨。 此时,船长和他的手下等我拿枪回去,已经丧失了耐心。 突然，霍西森船长出现在门口。 艾伦用宝剑指着他。

"越早开战，你就越早尝到宝剑穿身的滋味！"他喊道。

船长没对艾伦说一句话，只恶狠狠地看了我一眼。

"我会记住的，戴维。"他说。

过了一会儿，船长便走了。 艾伦左手抽出了一把匕首。

"你要沉着。"他说，"事已至此，难以挽回了，孩子。"

我爬到窗口，抱了好几支手枪，心跳得像一只鸟的心，既微弱又急促。 我感觉不到丝毫希望，只有一股憎恨世界的感觉。 进攻突然开始了———阵急促的脚步声，呐喊声，艾伦的一声大吼，然后便是他和舒安先生的击剑声。

"他害死了兰赛姆！"我大叫道。

"看好窗户！"艾伦喊道。

说这话时，他把宝剑刺进了舒安的身体。

透过窗户，我看到 5 个人扛着一块大木跑过。 他们试图用它将门毁坏。 我深吸一口气，向他们射击。 我一定击中了他们中的一个，因为其余 4 人停止了跑动。 我又射了两枪，他们都跑了。 现在后甲板室中弥漫着枪火烟雾。 艾伦站着等待，宝剑上沾满了血。

突然，更多的人冲着门奔来。 与此同时，天窗玻璃碎了，一个人跳进来。 我吓得没敢开枪。 我用手枪击打他的后脑勺，他却试图抓住我。 我恢复了勇气，向他开了一枪，然后射向天窗上的另一个家伙。 那个人掉落在他伙伴身上。

更多的人涌向门口。 艾伦的剑不停地挥动，每挥动一下就传来一个人的尖叫声，直到剩余的人跑掉。 艾伦用剑把 4 具水手尸体推出了后甲板室。

我几乎不能呼吸，两个被我射中的水手闪过眼前，如噩梦一般。 我开始像个小孩一样哽咽起来。

"你是个勇敢的小伙子，戴维。"艾伦亲切地说，"我会像爱护弟弟一样待你。 现在，睡会儿吧，我来站第一班岗。"

上午，艾伦从上衣上割下一个银纽扣。

"因为昨晚的作战，我送给你这个。"他说，"不论到哪里，你只要拿出这颗扣子，艾伦·布雷克的朋友就会帮助你。"

他刚说完，雷契先生就从外面向我们喊道：

"船长想要跟詹姆斯党人谈谈！"

艾伦向窗户走去。

"按我们说定的，带我去林尼湾！"艾伦生气地叫喊。

"好吧。"霍西森说，"但舒安死了，你们两位干的好事。 我们当中没人像他那样了解这处危险的海岸。 你能领航吗？"

"我更像个战士而不是水手，"艾伦回答；"不过我对这一带多少知道一些，我会帮你的。"

我们用一瓶白兰地交换了两桶清水，谈判就结束了。 艾伦和我坐了整整一天，讲述彼此的故事。 想不到，他告诉我他曾因为缺钱而参加英国军队，后来叛变成为一名詹姆斯党人。

"啊，天哪，"我说，"叛变是要以死刑作为惩罚的。 那你为何回到苏格兰呢？ 你来收集钱财吗？"

"我思念朋友和故乡。"艾伦叹息道，"我想看看荒野和麋鹿。 不过你猜对了，戴维，我是为部族首领阿希尔收集钱财才回来的。 卡洛登沼地战役中詹姆斯党人失败，他便逃到了法国。 现在他的苏格兰佃农不得不向乔治国王纳租，同时他们依然向阿希尔缴钱。"

"他们付双份地租呀！"我吃惊地说，"他们一定非常忠诚！"

我给艾伦讲了自己的一点事，说起坎贝尔先生如何把父亲的信交给我。

"我绝不会帮助姓坎贝尔的人。"艾伦气愤地说，"多年来，他们蹂躏我们部族，掠夺他们的土地。 最令人憎恨的是珂林·坎贝尔，因为他的红头发，我们叫他'红狐狸'……"

艾伦停了一会儿，好像因为过于愤怒而说不出话来。

"阿希尔逃到法国后，"艾伦继续说，"红狐狸请示乔治国王能否让他来收取阿希尔田地的租金。 如今，他已慢慢辞退了阿希尔所有的佃农。 若有机会逮到他，我……"

艾伦没有说下去。

那天我们没有再谈起这件事。 深夜，在清冷的天空下，大船撞到了礁石。 海浪翻上甲板，我们能听到脚下船体破碎的声响。

"我们在哪儿？"浪涛咆哮中，我冲艾伦喊道。

"姆尔海岸处。"他喊着回答，"坎贝尔族的地盘。"

我没来得及开口，一个巨浪把船抛起来，我被抛入了大海。

CHAPTER FOUR

The Murder of Red Fox

I do not know how many times I sank under the water. Just as I thought I would drown, I caught hold of a piece of wood. Soon, I floated into calmer water. Then, by kicking my legs, I came to the shore. And here I began the most unhappy part of my adventures.

As soon as it was morning, I climbed to the top of a hill and looked out to sea. I could not see the ship or my shipmates. I was on a small island, close to the Island of Mull. I started to walk across the island, looking for a way to get across to Mull itself.

On the second day, a fishing boat passed by, and the men on it shouted to me in Gaelic and laughed. Two days later, it came back and the men pointed towards Mull. At last, I understood.

"They're telling me I can walk to Mull when the tide is out," I thought. "How stupid I've been!"

I set off as soon as the tide was out. As soon as I reached the mainland, I came across an old gentleman, smoking his pipe in the sun.

"Have you seen any men from the ship out there?" I asked. "One of them was dressed like a gentleman. "

He shook his head.

"Was there one with a feathered hat?" I asked again.

He shook his head again.

"Are ye the lad with the silver button?" he asked at last.

"Why, yes!" I cried in surprise.

"Then I have a message for ye," he said. "Ye are to follow your friend to his country, to Appin."

I walked almost a hundred miles in the next four days, asking the way from everyone I met. At last, I came to the other side of Mull where I took a ferry over to the Scottish mainland. The boatman was called Neil Roy, one of Alan's clan, and I was keen to talk to him.

"I'm looking for somebody," I said. "Alan Breck Stewart's his name."

"The man you ask for is in France," Neil answered.

I remembered the silver button and showed it to him in the palm of my hand.

"Ye might have shown me the button straight away," he said. "But now all is well. I have been told to see that ye are safe."

I travelled on, remembering Neil Roy's advice — to speak to no one on the way, to avoid the Redcoats, and to hide in the bushes if any of them came. At last I came to the banks of Loch Linnhe.

I asked a fisherman to take me across the loch. Although it was only noon when we set out, the sky was dark, and the mountains around us were black and gloomy. On the other side of the loch, I sat thinking for a while.

"Am I doing the right thing?" I asked myself, "going to join an outlaw like Alan?"

Suddenly, four men came into view on the steep path below me — a large, red-headed gentlemen, a lawyer wearing a white wig, a servant and a sheriff's officer. I stepped out of the heather.

"Can you tell me the way to Appin?" I called to them.

They all stared at me in surprise.

"Who are ye looking for there?" the man with the red hair asked me.

"That's my business, sir," I told him.

As the man opened his mouth to reply, a shot came from the hill above me and he fell from his horse.

"I am dying! I am dying!" he cried.

I stared for a moment in horror. Then I ran up the hill, crying out, "Murderer! Murderer!" In the distance, I caught sight of a tall man in a black coat.

"Up here!" I shouted. "I can see him! Come up here! He's getting away!"

As I waited, a group of Redcoats came along the road.

"Ten pounds if ye take the lad!" the lawyer shouted to them. "He has helped to murder Colin Campbell."

Red Fox! Alan Breck's greatest enemy! My heart started to pound loudly. I stood frozen to the spot as I watched the soldiers spread out in the woods below me and raise their guns.

"Hide here," a man's voice whispered.

In the shelter of the trees I found Alan Breck.

第四章 "红狐狸" 之死

　　我不知沉入海水中多少次。 就在我以为自己要被淹死时，我抓住了一块木头。 不久，我漂进了一处比较平静的水域。 然后，凭借双腿不停地拍水，我上了岸。 从此我开始了险遇中最不愉快的经历。

　　天刚刚亮，我爬上一个小山顶向大海望去，却没有发现船和我的船友。 我所在的小岛靠近姆尔岛。 我开始步行穿越小岛，寻找通往姆尔岛的路径。

　　第二天，一艘渔船经过，船上的人用盖尔语冲我叫喊，然后大笑起来。 两天后，它驶回来，船上的人指了指姆尔岛。 最后，我明白了。

　　"他们是告诉我，退潮后我可以走着去姆尔岛。"我心想，"我真笨啊！"

　　潮水一退，我便起程了。 刚登上陆地，我遇到了一位老先生，他在阳光下抽烟。

　　"你见过那边航船上的人吗？"我问，"其中有一个人的穿着像一位绅士。"

　　他摇了摇头。

　　"有个帽子上带着羽毛的人吗？"我又问。

　　他再次摇头。

　　"你是拥有银纽扣的孩子吧？"他最后问道。

　　"啊，是！"我吃惊地喊道。

　　"那么我有消息给你，"他说，"你得追随你朋友去他家乡阿平。"

　　接下来的4天，我几乎行走了上百英里，向遇到的每一个人问路。 最后，我来到了姆尔岛的另一侧，在那里乘上了前往苏格兰本土的渡船。 船夫叫尼尔·罗伊，是艾伦部族里的一员，我急着想跟他说话。

"我在找一个人，"我说，"他叫艾伦·布雷克·斯图亚特。"

"你要找的人在法国。"尼尔回答。

我记起银纽扣，便放在手掌里给他看。

"你本该直接给我看这颗扣子的，"他说，"不过现在也没关系，我接受嘱托，要看着你平平安安的。"

我继续前行，记住了尼尔·罗伊的忠告——路上不要跟人讲话，避开红衣士兵，一旦碰到他们就躲到树丛中。 最后，我来到林尼湾岸边。

我请求一个船夫带我渡过海湾。 虽然我们出发时还是中午，可天空很暗，周围山脉也十分黑暗阴森。 渡到海湾对岸后，我坐着沉思了一阵。

"我正在做的事情正确吗？"我问自己，"要变成艾伦那样的逃犯吗？"

突然，4 个人出现在下边陡峭的道路上——一个魁梧的红发绅士、1 个头戴白色假发的律师、1 个仆人，还有 1 个执行官手下。 我从荒野里走出来。

"你们能告诉我如何去阿平吗？"我问他们。

他们都吃惊地盯着我。

"你去那里找谁？"红发的绅士问我。

"那是我自己的事，先生。"我告诉他。

此人刚要张嘴回答，一声枪响从我头顶上的山头传来，他应声落马。

"我快死了！ 我快死了！"他喊道。

我恐惧地望了一会儿，然后往山上跑去，大喊："谋杀了！ 谋杀了！"远处，我望见一个高大的黑衣人。

"来这里！"我嚷道，"我能看见他！ 爬上这里来！ 他要溜走了！"

我在等待着，一队红衣士兵沿路过来了。

"抓住那个孩子赏 10 磅！"律师冲他们喊道，"他参与谋杀了珂林·坎贝尔。"

红狐狸！ 艾伦·布雷克最大的敌人！ 我的心开始咚咚地跳着。 看到那些士兵在我下面的树林中散开并举起枪，我站着呆住了。

"藏到这儿。"一个男人低语道。

在树林隐蔽处，我发现了艾伦·布雷克。

CHAPTER FIVE

Journey to the Lowlands

Alan began to run through the trees and I followed him. Then we crawled through the heather. We couldn't stop and my heart seemed to be bursting against my ribs. I had no time to think, no breath to talk. A quarter of an hour later, Alan stopped and lay flat in the heather.

"Do as I do," he told me. "Your life depends on it."

Now we crawled back the way we had come, until we came to the wood where I had first found him. He lay, face down, in the bracken and panted like a dog. I lay beside him as if I were dead.

Alan was the first to get up. At first, I said nothing. The man that Alan hated was dead. And here was Alan hiding in the woods, running from the soldiers. Was my only friend in that wild country guilty?

"You and me cannot stay together," I told him angrily. "I like you very well, Alan, but your ways are not mine, and they're not God's. We must part."

"I'll not part from ye, David," Alan said, "until ye give me good reason. If ye ken something I don't, tell me."

"Alan," I said. "You know very well that Colin Campbell lies dead on the road down there."

"Did ever ye hear the story of the Man and the Good People?" Alan asked.

"No," I said, "and I don't want to hear it."

"I'll tell ye it, anyway, Mr Balfour," Alan said. "The Man was shipwrecked on a rock in the middle of the sea. He cried for his child, to see him one last time before he drowned. The Good People took pity on him. They brought the child in a bag and laid it beside the sleeping man. When the Man woke up, he saw the bag move. He was the sort of man who always thought the worst of things. So he stuck his dirk through the bag before he opened it. And there was his child — dead. Ye and that man are very much alike, Mr Balfour. "

"Do you mean that you did not kill Red Fox?" I asked.

"Mr Balfour of Shaws," Alan said, "if I were going to kill a Campbell, it would not be in my own country, to bring trouble on my clan."

He took out his dirk.

"And now I swear upon my holy dagger that I had no part in it."

I put out my hand, but he did not shake it.

"Alan," I said. "I offer you my hand for the second time."

We shook hands at last.

"How did you escape the shipwreck?" I asked.

"We managed to get into the small boat," Alan said, "and row to shore. Hoseason told the others to kill me and take my money to pay for the loss of his ship."

Alan's face turned very pale.

"It was seven to one, Davie," he said. "Then that little man... that officer..."

"Riach," I said.

"Ay, Riach," Alan answered. "He told me to run for it while he stopped the men from following. So I did. I didnae want to stay long there, not in Campbell country. I hoped ye were safe, Davie. I saw ye clinging to the wood. I told my friends to help ye if ye showed my silver button."

Alan stood up.

"We must leave this country now, David," he said. "The Redcoats will search the whole of Appin for me now. We must get to the Lowlands. We'll be safer there. Will ye come with me?"

"Ay, I'll go with you, Alan," I answered. "That's where I came from, and that's where I want to go back to. I want my uncle to be punished for what he's done."

"It will be hard," Alan said. "Ye'll have an empty belly. Your life will be like the hunted deer's and ye'll sleep with your hand upon your weapons. It's a life that I ken well. There's no other way. Either take to the heather with me, or hang for the murder of Red Fox."

As night fell, we started our long and dangerous journey.

第五章　低地之行

艾伦开始奔跑着在林中穿梭，我跟着他。 然后我们爬过了荒野。 我们不能停下，我的心仿佛胀得贴到了肋骨。 我没有时间思考，喘不过气，说不了话。 一刻钟后，艾伦停下脚步，平躺在荒野上。

"跟我做，"他告诉我，"你要活命就需要这样。"

此时，我们沿原路爬回，一直来到我当初发现艾伦的那块林地。 他面朝下趴着，脸埋在欧洲蕨里，像狗一样喘着气。 我躺在他旁边，像死了一样。

艾伦先坐起来，起初我没说话。 艾伦憎恨的人死了，而他正隐藏在这片树林中躲避士兵。 在这片荒野里我这唯一的朋友有罪吗？

"你我不能在一起了。"我气愤地告诉他，"我很喜欢你，艾伦。 但是你做事的方式与我不同，也不是上帝的方式。 我们必须分开。"

"我不会离开你的，戴维，"艾伦说，"除非你给出一个好理由。 如果你知道了什么事情而我不知道，请告诉我。"

"艾伦，"我说，"你很明白，珂林·坎贝尔死了，正躺在那边的路上呢。"

"你听说过'人和好人'的故事吗？"艾伦问道。

"没有，"我说，"我不想听。"

"不管怎样，我要讲给你听，鲍尔弗先生。"艾伦说，"有个人的船撞到大海中央的礁石上遇难了。 他哭得很伤心，希望在淹死前见他孩子最后一面。 '好人'同情他，他们用袋子把孩子带来，放到沉睡中的这个男人身边。 这人醒来时看到袋子在动，他是那种凡事往最坏处想的人，于是便用匕首狠狠戳了一下袋子。 打开一看，里面是他的孩子——已经死了。你和那人非常相像，鲍尔弗先生。"

"你的意思是你没有杀害红狐狸？"我问。

"肖家的鲍尔弗先生，"艾伦说，"我若想杀坎贝尔家的人，就不会在我的家乡动手，那样会给我的部族带来麻烦。"

他拔出匕首。

"现在，我对这把神圣的匕首起誓，我绝没有参与此事。"

我伸出手，他却没有握。

"艾伦，"我说，"我再次向你伸出手。"

我们最终握手了。

"你是如何逃离失事船只的？"我问。

"我们成功登上了一艘小船，"艾伦说，"划到岸边。 霍西森让其他的人杀死我，还要拿走我的钱财以赔偿船的损失。"

艾伦的脸色变得非常苍白。

"他们7对1，戴维，"他说，"然后，那个小个子……那个船员……"

"雷契，"我说。

"是的，雷契，"艾伦回答道，"他让我逃跑，而他为我阻挡前来追赶的家伙，我因此逃了命。 我不想长久待在那里，不愿待在坎贝尔的地盘上。 我希望你是安全的，戴维。 我看见你抱住了木头。 我告诉朋友们，如果你给他们看我的银纽扣，就要帮助你。"

艾伦站起来。

"现在我们必须离开我的家乡，戴维。"他说，"如今，红衣士兵为找我将搜遍整个阿平。 我们必须去低地，那里更安全。 你要跟我去吗？"

"是的，我会跟你一起，艾伦。"我回答，"我从那里来的，也想回到那里。 我要让叔叔为他的所作所为受到惩罚。"

"一路上会很艰难的。"艾伦说，"你要饿着肚子，你会活得像一只被捕猎的鹿一般，睡觉时手中都要握着武器。 那种生活我很清楚，但别无选择了。 或者跟我前往荒野，或者因谋杀红狐狸而被绞死。"

夜幕降临，我们开始了漫长而危险的旅程。

CHAPTER SIX

Danger on the Rocks

At first, we walked over rough mountain-sides, towards the house of James Stewart, Ardshiel's half-brother who collected the money for Alan to take back to France. At about half-past ten, we came to the top of a brae and saw the lights of a house below us. Six or seven people were moving about outside.

"If we were Redcoats," Alan said, "James would be in terrible trouble."

Alan whistled three times as we came down to the yard. A tall, handsome man of more than fifty, called out in Gaelic.

"James Stewart," Alan answered him, "this is David Balfour, a young gentleman of the Lowlands. He doesnae speak Gaelic."

James greeted me politely, then turned back to Alan.

"The Campbell murder will bring us trouble," he said.

"Colin Campbell's dead," Alan replied. "Thank God for that."

"Ay," James said, "and I wish he was alive again. The murder took place here in Appin and we'll all pay the price. I'm afraid for my family."

While they were talking, I watched people taking guns out from under the thatched roofs and burying them on the hill-side. James gave us swords and pistols, and food and brandy. Then he asked us to leave.

"If the Redcoats ken you've been here, I'll hang," he said.

"Can ye give us money?" Alan asked.

"I've none," James said, "but I'll find some for ye. Go and hide and send me word where ye are. "

Darkness was falling as we set off again. Sometimes we walked, sometimes we ran. Although the countryside seemed empty, there were houses everywhere, hidden in the quiet places of the hills so we travelled only at night.

One evening, we had to cross a fast-flowing river. Alan jumped onto a rock in the middle of the water and I followed him. I looked down at the water between us and the river bank and I started to tremble. I put my hand over my eyes. Alan shook me angrily but I could not move. He forced me to drink some brandy, shouted, "Hang or drown!" then jumped safely to the other side of the river.

I was now alone on the rock.

"It's now or never!" I thought.

I flung myself forward. Only my hands caught hold of the rock. Alan held onto my collar and dragged me in. He did not speak, but started running. I staggered to my feet and stumbled after him, tired and bruised.

At last, Alan stopped under an enormous rock. He climbed to the top, pulling me after him, and we lay flat, looking all around us. It was a clear dawn and we could see the stony sides of the valley. There were no houses anywhere, and it was silent except for the eagles screeching around the mountain tops. Alan smiled.

"Now we have a chance," he said. "Ye're not very good at this jumping, are ye, David?"

I blushed.

"No blame to ye!" he laughed. "You did what ye were afraid of. That's the best kind of man. And I'm to blame for having nae water with us, only brandy!"

"Empty out the brandy," I said, "then I'll go down to the river and fill the bottle. "

Alan shook his head.

"I wouldnae waste it," he said. "Now sleep, lad, I'll keep watch."

I woke up at about nine in the morning. It was cloudless and very hot.

"Ye were snoring," Alan told me, his face anxious.

"Does that matter?" I asked.

"Ay, it does," he said. "Look down there."

I peered over the edge of the rock and gasped in surprise. About half-a-mile up the river was a Redcoat camp. On the top of a rock stood a sentry and there were other sentries all along the river. In the distance were soldiers on horse-back.

"This is what I was afraid of, Davie," Alan said. "They're watching the burn-side. We'll try to get past them tonight."

"And what are we to do until then?" I asked.

"Hide here," he said.

We lay on top of that rock, like scones baking over a fire. The little patch of earth and fern was only big enough for one, so we took turns to lie there. We had no water, but we kept the brandy as cool as we could.

And all this time the soldiers made their way along the valley towards us, prodding the heather with their bayonets. My blood ran cold at the sight of them. Then they started to climb the slopes of the mountain. Suddenly, there were soldiers all around the bottom of our rock as they sat down to rest.

I almost stopped breathing with fear.

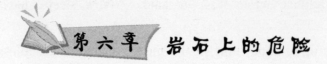

第六章 岩石上的危险

首先，我们爬过崎岖的山坡，前往詹姆斯·斯图亚特家，阿希尔同父异母的兄弟收集了钱财，让艾伦带回法国。10点半左右，我们来到斜坡顶上，看到下边一座房子里亮着灯光，六七个人在外面奔来奔去。

"如果我们是一帮红衣士兵，"艾伦说，"詹姆斯家就遇上大麻烦了。"

我们来到下面的院子时，艾伦吹了3声口哨。一个50多岁、相貌堂堂的高个男子用盖尔语大声招呼着。

"詹姆斯·斯图亚特，"艾伦回应他，"这是戴维·鲍尔弗，来自低地的一位年轻绅士。他不会说盖尔语。"

詹姆斯很有礼貌地向我问好，然后转向艾伦。

"坎贝尔被杀将给我们带来麻烦。"他说。

"珂林·坎贝尔死了，"艾伦回答，"为此感谢上帝。"

"是啊，"詹姆斯说，"我希望他能活过来，谋杀发生在阿平，我们是要付出代价的。我为家族担忧啊。"

他们谈话时，我看到人们从茅草屋顶下拿出枪埋到山坡上。詹姆斯给了我们剑、手枪、食物和白兰地，随后他让我们离开。

"如果红衣士兵知道你们来过这里，我会被绞死的。"他说。

"能给我们些钱吗？"艾伦问。

"我没有，"詹姆斯说，"但我会为你们找一些。先离开，找个地方避避，然后捎口信告诉我你们在哪儿。"

我们再次上路时，夜幕已降临。我们时而行走，时而奔跑。虽然这一带看似空旷，山岭僻静处却隐藏着一间间房屋，因此我们只能夜间赶路。

一天晚上，我们不得不渡过一条湍急的河流。艾伦跳到河水中央的一块岩石上，我跟随着他。我低头看看两岸间的水流，便开始发抖，并用手遮住了眼睛。艾伦生气地摇着我，我却动不了。他给我灌了些白兰地，大喝一声："想绞死还是淹死！"然后他安全跳到河流的彼岸。

此时我独自站在岩石上。

"现在不跳，就永远别想再跳了！"我心想。

我使劲向前一跳，只有双手抓住了岩石。 艾伦抓住我的衣领，把我拖上岸。 他一句话也没说，而是开始奔跑。 我摇摇晃晃地站起来，踉踉跄跄跟着他，十分疲惫，而且擦伤了。

最后，艾伦停在一块巨大的岩石下面。 他先爬到顶上，又把我拉上去。我们平躺在上边，四处查看。 天色已经明亮，我们可以看到山谷的石壁。四处没有房屋，一片寂静，只有几只苍鹰在山顶周围鸣叫。 艾伦微笑了。

"现在我们有一点希望了，"他说，"你不擅长跳跃，对吧，戴维？"我脸红了。

"不是责怪你！"他笑起来，"你做了让你感到害怕的事，是个了不起的人啊。 该受责备的人是我，没带水，只有白兰地！"

"把白兰地倒出来，"我说，"然后我到河边灌满一瓶。"
艾伦摇摇头。

"我不想浪费酒，"他说，"现在睡觉吧，孩子，我来守望。"
大约早上9点钟，我醒了，天空无云而且很热。

"你打鼾了。"他告诉我，满脸焦虑的样子。

"有什么关系吗？"我问道。

"是的，"他说，"看看下边。"

顺着岩石边缘望去，我惊骇地吸了口气。 离河流大约半英里处，有一处红衣士兵的营地。 那边岩石顶上有一个哨兵，沿河流还分布着很多岗哨，远处则是骑马的士兵。

"这正是我所担心的，戴维。"艾伦说，"他们监视着小溪。 我们今晚要设法通过。"

"那晚上之前我们要干什么呢？"我问。

"藏在这里。"他说。

我俩躺在岩石顶上，就像火上烘烤的烙饼。 一小块长着蕨类的泥土地面只够一个人的面积，所以我们轮流躺在那里。 我们没有一滴水，却尽力保持着白兰地的清凉。

士兵们一直在我们附近的河谷处转来转去，用刺刀在灌木丛中乱刺。一看到他们，我的血液就冰冷下来。 然后他们开始爬向山坡。 突然，我们所在的岩石底部围满了坐下休息的士兵。

我吓得几乎停止了呼吸。

CHAPTER SEVEN

Wanted: Dead or Alive

*W*e lay there for two hours. It was only luck and the hot sun that saved us.

"We should go now," Alan whispered at last, "while they're asleep."

We slipped from one rock to the other, crawling flat on our bellies, then making a run for it. Most of the soldiers, still sleepy in the sun, stayed down by the river. We slowly got away from them, although we could still see the sentry on the rock.

At last we came to a burn and plunged ourselves into its cool water. Then we mixed oatmeal with it and ate — a good enough dish for a hungry man.

We moved on quickly again that night. It was a difficult path — up the sides of high mountains and along steep cliffs. I was afraid all the time. It was still dark when we reached our destination — a cleft in the great mountain with water running through it. There were caves and woods and trout in the stream. We even dared to light a fire. It was here that Alan taught me how to use a sword.

"We've been here for five days," Alan said one day. "I must send word to James. Could ye lend me my button, Davie?"

I gave him the silver button. He tied it to a little cross of twigs.

"There's a friend of mine living not far from here — John Breck," he said, "and I can trust him with my life. Ye see, David, there will be a reward for us now, dead or alive. So I cannae show my face, even to go to my friends. But when it's dark, I'll leave my silver button. "

"And what will John Breck do when he finds it?" I asked.

"In our clan, this cross is the signal for a meeting," he told me, "but since there's no letter with it, he kens that cannae be. But he will ken there is something wrong. When he sees my button, he'll think, 'Alan Breck is in the heather, and has need of me.'"

"But there's a great deal of heather," I said. "How will he find us?"

"True," Alan answered, "but then he'll see the birch and the pine twigs, and he'll ken where to come. "

"Would it not be simpler to write?" I asked.

"That is an excellent idea, Mr Balfour of Shaws," Alan said, "it certainly would be simpler. But it would be very difficult for John Breck to read it. He would have to go to school to learn first. "

That night, Alan placed his cross in John Breck's window. About noon the next day, we saw a man coming up the side of the mountain, guided by Alan's whistling. John Breck was a ragged, bearded man, with terrible smallpox scars on his face. He took Alan's message and left straight away.

It was three days before John Breck came back. He brought bad news — everybody was saying that Alan had murdered Colin Campbell, the countryside was alive with Redcoats looking for him and James Stewart was already in prison accused of helping in the murder.

"Can it get any worse?" Alan asked.

John Breck unrolled a poster sent by James's wife.

WANTED

A SMALL MAN, POCK-MARKED
SKIN, OF ABOUT THIRTY-FIVE, DRESSED IN
A FEATHERED HAT, A FRENCH COAT OF
BLUE WITH SILVER BUTTONS AND LACE,
A RED WAISTCOAT AND BREECHES OF BLACK
VELVET. HE IS WITH A TALL STRONG LAD OF
ABOUT EIGHTEEN, WEARING A RAGGED
BLUE COAT, AN OLD HIGHLAND BONNET,
A LONG WAISTCOAT, BLUE BREECHES, BARE
LEGS, HEAVY SHOES WITH HOLES AT THE
TOES, SPEAKS LIKE A LOWLANDER, AND
HAS NO BEARD.

Then John Breck took out his purse and took out four guineas in gold, and another in small change.

"I thank ye," Alan said, putting the coins in his pocket. "And now, John Breck, if ye will hand over my button, we'll be off again."

Eleven hours of hard travelling over a range of high mountains brought us right to the edge of a wide moor. Alan looked at me, his face pale and worried.

"It's not a good place, Davie, lad," he said, "but we have to cross it."

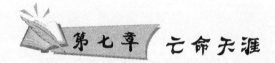

第七章　亡命天涯

我们在那里躺了 2 个小时，只是靠侥幸和灼热的太阳救了我们。

"我们现在应该离开，"艾伦终于小声说，"他们睡着了。"

我们从一块块岩石旁溜过去，肚子贴着地面爬行，随后奔跑着逃离。多数士兵还在太阳底下睡眼惺忪地站在岸边的岗位上。我们慢慢远离了他们，只是依旧可以看到岩石上的岗哨。

最后，我们来到一处小溪旁，跳进了清凉的水中。然后，我们用冷水拌麦片粥吃起来——对饥饿的人而言，这已是丰盛的一餐。

那晚我们又开始快速前行。道路异常难行——要攀爬高高的山坡和陡峭的悬崖。我始终心存担忧。天色依旧阴暗，我们抵达了目的地——一个山顶上的裂口。裂口处淌过一条河，处处可见洞穴、树林，河里还有鳟鱼。我们甚至很大胆地生起了火，在这里艾伦教会了我使用剑。

"我们来这儿已经 5 天了，"一天，艾伦说，"我必须给詹姆斯捎个口信。能把银纽扣借给我吗，戴维？"

我把银纽扣给了他。他将纽扣系到树枝做成的小十字架上。

"我的一个朋友住得离这里不远——叫约翰·布雷克，"他说，"我可以把自己的生命托付给他。 你知道的，戴维，人们正悬赏捉拿我们呢，不论生死，所以我不能露面，甚至不能去朋友那里。 但天黑时，我会把银纽扣留给他。"

"约翰·布雷克发现银纽扣后会怎样做呢？"我问。

"在我们部族，十字架是集合的信号。"他告诉我，"因为没有附带信件，所以他不会这样想。 不过，他会知道事情不妙。 他看到我的扣子，就会猜想'艾伦·布雷克在荒野里，需要我的帮助。'"

"可是有很多荒野，"我说，"他如何找到我们呢？"

"的确如此。"艾伦回答，"但如果他看到桦树枝和松树枝，就能知道应前往哪里了。"

"写字不是更加简单吗？"我问。

"那是个好主意，肖家的鲍尔弗先生。"艾伦说，"那当然更简单。 不过，让约翰·布雷克读懂却很难，他还得先入学读书才行。"

那晚，艾伦将十字架放到了约翰·布雷克家的窗口。 次日中午时分，我们看到有个人向山这边走来，艾伦吹起口哨为他引路。 约翰·布雷克衣着破烂，蓄着胡须，脸上长着恐怖的麻痕。 他带上艾伦的消息就立刻离开了。

3 天过后，约翰·布雷克才回来。 他带回了坏消息——每个人都说艾伦杀死了珂林·坎贝尔，家乡到处都是寻找艾伦的红衣士兵，詹姆斯·斯图亚特已经被指控为帮凶并被关进了监狱。

"还有更坏的消息吗？"艾伦问道。

约翰·布雷克打开了一张詹姆斯的妻子送来的海报。

通　缉

矮个男子，面部长有麻点，

年约 35 岁，头戴插有羽毛的

帽子，身穿缝有银纽扣和花边

的法式蓝色上衣、一件红

色马甲和粗毛绒的黑色骑马裤。

伙伴是年约 18 岁、身强力壮的
高个少年，穿一件蓝色的破旧
外套，戴一顶高地式旧圆帽，
穿着长马甲、蓝色的骑马裤，
露着腿，沉重的鞋子上脚趾处
有洞，带有低地口音，
没有胡子。

然后，约翰·布雷克拿出他的钱包，取出 4 枚金几尼，剩下的全是零钱。

"我谢谢你。"艾伦说着把钱放进了口袋，"现在，约翰·布雷克，如果你还给我扣子，我们就要再次上路了。"

沿着高山行走 11 个小时后，我们来到了一处大沼泽地的边缘。 艾伦看着我，他脸色苍白，忧虑起来。

"这可不是一处好地方，戴维，伙计，"他说，"但我们必须穿过去。"

CHAPTER EIGHT

Escape Across the Moor

As we stood there, the mist rose away from the moor and showed us the countryside we had to cross. Most of it was red with heather and some was blackened by fire. Here and there, it was dotted with dead fir trees, standing like skeletons.

"But if we cross it, the Redcoats will see us if they come across the mountain," I said.

"If we go back, we'll hang," Alan said softly.

"It's all a risk," I said. "Let's go ahead."

Alan was delighted.

"Ye're a brave lad, Davie," he said.

We came slowly down the mountain-side and slipped into the heather. For most of the time we crawled from one clump of heather to another, like hunters tracking the deer. It was another hot day and we had no water left in the brandy bottle.

We took it in turns to sleep and to watch for soldiers. But I fell asleep when I was on guard. By the time I woke up, a group of soldiers had already come down the hill-side. They were making their way towards us, spread out in the shape of a fan.

"I've let us down," I whispered to Alan, ashamed. "What can we do now?"

He pointed to a high mountain ahead of us, to the north-east.

"We'll try to get over to Ben Alder," he said.

"But we'll have to cross right in front of the soldiers!" I said.

"I ken that," he said, "and ye ken that if we turn back to Appin, we're dead men!"

As Alan spoke, he began to run through the heather on his hands and knees. I followed him as quickly as I could. A thin choking dust rose from the ground as we moved, drying our throats even more. Only my fear of letting Alan down again made me carry on.

At dusk, we heard the sound of a trumpet and the soldiers stopped to set up camp in the middle of the moor.

"There'll be no sleep for us tonight!" Alan whispered. "When day comes, we'll be safe on the mountain."

"I can't go on, Alan," I gasped.

"Very well, then, I'll carry ye," Alan said.

"No," I whispered. "Lead the way."

The night was cool and dark. A heavy dew fell and drenched the moor like rain and we wet our lips with it. I thought of nothing else but the next step. And I thought that each one would be my last.

When day dawned, we were far enough away from the soldiers to walk instead of crawl. But our troubles were not over.

As we walked, four men jumped out of the heather and held their dirks to our throats.

第八章　沼泽逃亡

我们站在那里，沼泽地上的迷雾已经散去，展现在眼前的是我们必须穿越的荒原。 这儿多半是红色的石楠，还有一些被火烧成了黑色。 到处点缀着死去的枞木，它们像骷髅一样耸立着。

"但如果我们穿越这里，红衣士兵到山上就会发现我们。"我说。

"倘若回去，我们将被绞死。"艾伦轻轻说道。

"既然都是冒险，"我说，"我们还是前进吧。"

艾伦很高兴。

"你是个勇敢的孩子，戴维。"他说。

我们慢慢走下山坡，逃入了荒原。 大部分时间里，我们从一个石楠爬到另一个石楠，就像猎人们追踪鹿一样。 又是炎热的一天，我们白兰地瓶子里已经空空如也。

我们轮流睡觉，轮流守望敌人。 我看守时却睡着了，醒来时，一队士兵已从山坡上走下来。 他们逐渐逼近我们，散布成扇形。

"我让你失望了。"我惭愧地对艾伦低语，"现在我们该怎么办？"

他指了指我们前面东北方向的一座高山。

"我们要设法翻过那座山，去本·亚尔德。"他说。

"那么，我们必须在士兵前面翻过去啊！"我说。

"我知道。"他说，"你明白，若回阿平，我们只有死路一条！"

艾伦说着，爬着穿行在石楠丛中，我紧随其后。 我们爬行着，尘土扬起，十分呛人，令我们的喉咙更加干燥。 只因害怕再次让艾伦失望，我坚持跑着。

黄昏时分，我们听到了号声，士兵们停止了搜索，在荒原中央扎起了帐篷。

"今夜我们不能睡了！"艾伦小声说，"天亮时，我们就能安全到达山上。"

"我走不动了，艾伦。"我气喘吁吁地说。

"好吧，那我来背你。"艾伦说。

"不用，"我低声说，"你带路吧。"

夜晚凉快而黑暗，浓浓的露水降下来，像雨水一样浸透了沼泽，也滋润着我们的嘴唇。 除了爬动下一步，我什么也不想。 每挪动一步，我都以为那将是自己的最后一步。

天放亮时，我们已经离士兵很远，可以走路而无需爬行了。 然而我们的麻烦并未结束。

我们正走着，从灌木丛中跳出4个人，手持匕首顶着我们的喉咙。

CHAPTER NINE

The Quarrel

Alan whispered to the men in Gaelic and they put away their weapons — but they took ours, too.

"Don't worry," Alan said, "they're Cluny Macpherson's men. He's been one of the leaders of the Jacobite rebellion for years. I thought he was still in France."

The men invited us to visit Cluny's hiding-place, which was perched on the edge of a mountain. He was pleased to see us.

"Bonnie Prince Charlie hid here with me once," he boasted.

It was a long and tiring evening for me. I could not understand a word of the conversation because everybody spoke Gaelic. I soon fell into a deep sleep. I can remember only one thing about that strange evening— Alan lost all our money playing cards. In the morning, Cluny gave it back to us. I did not want it, for I felt that it had been fairly won, but I had to swallow my pride and take it.

Two days later, one of Cluny's men took us across Loch Ericht and on to Loch Rannoch. From there, Alan and I travelled towards the head of the River Forth, in the Lowlands. It was a terrible journey. At night, we crossed high mountains in heavy rain and fierce winds. By day, we lay and slept in the wet heather. It was often misty and we lost our way more than once.

I felt so ill that I wanted to die. And I was so angry with Alan for gambling with our money that we hardly spoke until the third night.

"Let me carry your pack," he said.

"I can carry it, thank you," I said coldly.

"I'll not offer again, David," he said. "I'm not a patient man."

"I never said you were," I answered, as silly and as rude as a boy of ten.

I knew that I was wrong to be so unforgiving, but I could not help it. Then Alan began to whistle a Jacobite tune.

"Just you remember that my king is King George!" I said angrily.

"And I am a Stewart!" he answered, "the same name as my king!"

"I saw many Stewarts while I was in the Highlands," I said, "and they would all be better for a good wash!"

"Do ye know that ye insult me?" Alan asked fiercely.

I pulled out my sword as Alan had taught me. Alan pulled out his sword, too. There was a long silence.

"I cannae fight ye," Alan said at last. He threw his sword onto the ground. "Nae, nae, I cannae."

The anger drained out of me. I felt sick and dizzy and I thought that I was dying.

"I can't breathe properly," I gasped. "If I die, Alan, will you forgive me for what I said?"

Alan picked me up and carried me on his back. We were friends again at last.

第九章　争　吵

艾伦用盖尔语和他们轻声交谈，他们收起了武器——但同时拿走了我们的武器。

"不必担心，"艾伦说，"他们是克伦努·麦克华逊的手下。 多年来，他一直是詹姆斯党反抗者的领袖之一，我本以为他还在法国呢。"

他们带我们来到克伦努的藏身处———一座山崖上。 见到我们他很高兴。

"邦尼·查理王子曾和我一起躲在这里呢。"他夸口道。

对我来说，那一夜既漫长又令人疲惫，他们的谈话我一个字也听不懂，因为每个人都说着盖尔语。 我很快便睡熟了，只记得那个莫名之夜发生过一件事——艾伦打牌时输掉了我们所有的钱。 早晨，克伦努把钱还给我们。 我本不想要，因为我觉得钱他们赢得公平，可是我还得收起自尊心，接受了这笔钱。

两天后，克伦努的一个手下带我们渡过爱洛特湖，来到蓝诺其湖。 从那里出发，艾伦和我前往位于低地的福司河源头。 那是一次可怕的历程。夜晚，我们冒着暴风骤雨翻越山岭。 白天，我们就躺在湿湿的野地中睡觉。 天经常下雾，我们不止一次迷了路。

我感觉很难受，想死掉算了。 艾伦用我们的钱赌博，我对他非常生气，第三天晚上之前，我们几乎没说话。

"我给你背包吧。"他说。

"我能背，谢谢。"我冷冷地说。

"我不会再主动帮忙了，戴维。"他说，"我可不是一个有耐心的人。"

"我也没说过你有耐心啊。"我答道，愚蠢而粗鲁，像个 10 岁的孩子。

我明白自己这样不饶人是不对的，却无法控制自己。 这时，艾伦吹起一支詹姆斯党人的调子。

"你要记住，我的国王是乔治！"我愤愤地说。

"我姓斯图亚特！"他回答，"跟我的国王同姓！"

"在高地时我见到了很多斯图亚特人。"我说，"他们都需要好好清洗一下。"

"你可知道你这是在侮辱我？"艾伦愤怒地问。

我照艾伦教我的那样拔出了剑。 艾伦也拔出了他的剑。 沉默了很久。

"我不能跟你打。"艾伦最后说。 他把剑扔到地上，说："不，不，我不能。"

我的怒气消了。 我感到难受，头晕眼花，认为自己快死了。

"我无法正常呼吸。"我喘息着，"如果我死了，艾伦，你能原谅我所说的话吗？"

艾伦把我扶起来，背着我，我们终于又成了朋友。

CHAPTER TEN

Back to the House of Shaws

*F*or the rest of July and into August, Alan and I travelled on into the Lowlands. I decided that I would go and see Mr Rankeillor in Queensferry. I knew that he was my uncle's lawyer, but I did not know what else to do.

"I should be able to trust him," I told myself. "He's a lawyer. I'll tell him how my uncle had me kidnapped."

At last, I left Alan in hiding to walk into Queensferry. The sun was just coming up. I did not ask the way because I was so ashamed of my dirty appearance. Instead, I walked up and down strange streets, like a dog looking for its master. After a while, I saw a man coming out of a fine tall house. He looked strangely at me.

"What are you doing here, boy?" he asked.

"I'm here on business, sir," I replied. "I'm looking for Mr Rankeillor's house."

"I am Mr Rankeillor," he said.

I took a deep breath to stop myself from trembling.

"My name is David Balfour," I said. "I should like to speak to you in private, sir."

To my relief, Mr Rankeillor did not send me away. He took me into his house and I started to tell him my story.

"The ship sank, sir, and. . ."

"I heard about the shipwreck," Mr Rankeillor said, "but that was on the 27 June! Today is the 24 August. Where have you been?"

"If I tell you, I shall have to mention a friend. "

Mr Rankeillor looked worried.

"Do not mention any Highlander names to me, " he said. "Many of them have broken the law. Call your friend. . . er. . . Mr Thompson. "

How kind Mr Rankeillor was! When I had finished speaking, he fed me and gave me clean clothes. I slowly came back to life.

"I knew your father, David, " he said later. "He and your uncle were in love with the same woman — your mother. They came to an agreement. Your father married her and moved to Essendean. Ebenezer kept the family estate, the house of Shaws, near Edinburgh. It is yours now by law. "

"But my father was the younger brother, " I said in surprise. "Surely it belongs to my uncle?"

"No, David, " Mr Rankeillor said. "Your father was the elder brother. You inherit everything on his death. Your uncle knew that. "

"So that's why he tried to kill me, " I whispered.

"It would be better to settle this matter privately, " Mr Rankeillor said. "Otherwise, your friendship with. . . er. . . Mr Thompson might be a problem. "

I thought about it for a long time.

"Mr Rankeillor, " I said at last, "I have an idea. . . "

It was dark when Alan, Mr Rankeillor, his clerk and myself reached the house of Shaws. No lights shone from its windows, and I shuddered as I remembered the night in June when I came there alone.

Alan walked up to the door and knocked loudly as we hid in the bushes. The window above the door opened with a clatter.

"What's this?" my uncle shouted. "What brings ye here at this time of the night？"

"David，" Alan said.

My uncle came to the door slowly, holding a gun.

"I have a friend who lives near the Island of Mull，" Alan said. "A ship was wrecked there in June. My friend found a young boy, half-drowned, on the sands — your nephew, David Balfour. "

Alan paused and stared at my uncle.

"I've come with a message. Do ye want the lad killed or kept？"

"They'll get no money from me，" my uncle shouted.

"Killed or kept？" Alan repeated.

There was a long silence.

"Kept，" my uncle muttered. "We'll have naemore bloodshed. "

I stepped out of the bushes.

"Good evening, uncle，" I said.

And as Mr Rankeillor appeared next to me, my uncle stood clutching his gun like a man turned to stone. We went into the house where my uncle and the lawyer talked late into the night. By the time I went to bed, it was agreed that my uncle would pay me two thirds of his income from the estate of the house of Shaws. I lay until dawn, watching the flames flicker on the ceiling of my room and planning my future now that I was a rich man.

And Alan？ He is waiting for a ship to take him to France. I dread him going, for I do not think that I shall ever find such a good friend again.

第十章 重回肖家

过完 7 月剩余的日子，进入 8 月初，艾伦和我一直走到了低地。 我决定去看望皇后码头的兰基勒先生。 我知道他是叔叔的律师，却不知还能做什么。

"我应该信任他。"我告诉自己，"他是一名律师。 我要告诉他，叔叔是如何将我拐卖的。"

最后，我从藏身处离开艾伦，走向皇后码头。 太阳快要升起来了，我一直没有问路，因为我为自己蓬头垢面而感到惭愧。 相反，我走在高低起伏的陌生街道上，就像一只寻找主人的狗。 一会儿后，我看见一个人从一幢漂亮高大的房子里走出来。 他奇怪地望着我。

"你到这里做什么，孩子？"他问。

"我到这里办事，先生。"我回答，"我在寻找兰基勒先生家。"

"我就是兰基勒先生。"他说。

我深吸一口气，不让自己颤抖。

"我叫戴维·鲍尔弗。"我说，"我想和你私下谈谈，先生。"

令我欣喜的是，兰基勒先生没有赶我走。 他把我带到家中，我开始给他讲述自己的故事。

"船沉没了，先生，然后……"

"我听说过船失事，"兰基勒先生说，"但那发生在 6 月 27 日啊！ 今天是 8 月 24 日，你去哪里了？"

"若要讲给你听，我不得不提及一个朋友。"

兰基勒先生看似很担忧。

"不要向我提及任何高地人的名字。"他说，"他们中的很多人触犯了法律。 把你那位朋友称作……呃……汤姆逊先生吧。"

兰基勒先生多么亲切啊！ 我讲完后，他给我吃的，还送我干净的衣服。 我慢慢恢复了过来。

"我认识你父亲，戴维。"他后来说，"他和你叔叔爱上了同一个女人——你母亲。 他们达成了一项协议。 你父亲娶了她并迁往埃森底，而埃比尼泽经营着家产，即爱丁堡附近的肖家。 依据法律，家产现在是你的了。"

"可我父亲是弟弟呀。"我吃惊地说,"家产当然属于叔叔啊?"

"不,戴维,"兰基勒先生说,"你父亲是哥哥。 他死后你应继承所有家产,你叔叔明白这一点。"

"怪不得他要想方设法杀害我呢。"我低语。

"私下解决这件事会更好,"兰基勒先生说,"否则,可能给那位……呃……汤姆逊先生带来麻烦。"

我思考了很长时间。

"兰基勒先生,"我最后说,"我有个主意……"

天黑时,艾伦、兰基勒先生、他的书记员和我一起来到肖家。 窗内没有灯光,想起6月独自前来的那一夜,我就发抖。

艾伦走到门前,把门敲得很响,我们则藏在灌木丛中。 门上的窗户咔嗒一声打开了。

"是谁?"我叔叔大喊,"这么晚了,谁让你来的?"

"戴维。"艾伦说。

我叔叔慢慢走到门口,拿着一把枪。

"我有个朋友住在姆尔岛附近。"艾伦说,"6月份,那里失事了一艘船。 我朋友发现了一个年轻男孩,他淹得半死,在沙滩上——那是你的侄子,戴维·鲍尔弗。"

艾伦停了停,盯着我叔叔。

"我带来一个口信儿。 你想要那孩子死呢还是留着他?"

"他们休想从我这里拿到任何钱财。"我叔叔吆喝说。

"是让他死还是留着他。"艾伦重复道。

沉寂了很久。

"留着他。"叔叔咕哝着,"我们不想再流血。"

我走出灌木丛。

"晚上好啊,叔叔。"我说。

兰基勒先生随后出现在我身旁,我叔叔握着枪站着,仿佛变成了一尊石像。 我们走进房屋,叔叔和律师一直谈到深夜。 我上床睡觉时,已经达成一项协议,叔叔要付给我他从肖家所得收入的三分之二。 我一直躺到天亮,望着屋顶上闪烁的光芒,计划着成为富人后的未来。

艾伦呢? 他在等待一艘船带他去法国。 我很不愿意他离开,因为我觉得自己再也遇不到这样的挚友了。